First Aladdin Books edition 1990

Aladdin Books
Macmillan Publishing Company
866 Third Avenue, New York, NY 10022

First published 1990 in Great Britain
by Walker Books Ltd, London.

Printed by South China Printing Co. (1988) Ltd., Hong Kong

10 9 8 7 6 5 4 3 2 1

BOMC offers recordings and compact discs, cassettes
and records. For information and catalog write to
BOMR, Camp Hill, PA 17012.

Library of Congress Cataloging-in-Publication Data
Radford, Derek.
  Harry builds a house / Derek Radford.–1st Aladdin Books ed.
     p.   cm
  Summary; Harry Hippo and his friends build a house, step by step from
digging a ditch for the pipes to putting in the last joints and plugs.
  ISBN 0–689–71439–4
  [1. House construction—Fiction. 2. Hippopotamus—Fiction.]
  I. Title.
PZ7.R116Har   1990
[E]– dc20   90–187
                                                                                CIP
                                                                                 AC

Derek Radford

Aladdin Books
Macmillan Publishing Company
New York

Harry Hippo is building a new house.
First he maps out the site.

Then a bulldozer clears the land and makes sure it is level.

A backhoe is used to make
a long ditch. Then the pipes
for the drains are laid
in it and fitted together.

Once the pipes are laid the ditch is covered over again and flattened with a bulldozer. Next a road is built to the site.

Now work on the house can begin.
Harry and the builders look at the plan.

They measure out the ground and put
in pegs to mark where the walls will go.

Some of the machines
and materials to be used:

payloader

wrench

tool box

bucket

hard hat

concrete blocks

telephone

sand

dump truck

forklift
truck

bricks

loader

The first job is to lay the
foundations, because the
house must sit on something
firm and solid.

Dump trucks bring concrete from
the mixer and tip it into the trench.
Large covers are put over the
concrete at night to keep it dry
so it will set hard and firm.

Wherever a wall will be
built a trench is dug out.

When the foundations are laid the wall building can begin. Harry uses bricks for the outside walls and concrete blocks for the inside walls.

trowel

pointing trowel

bucket

brush

string

mortar board

mason's level

These are some of the bricklayers' tools.

The bricklayers make sure that windows and door frames are in the right place.

The mortar is mixed; this will hold the bricks together.

Newly laid bricks are checked to make sure they are level.

Now the scaffolding arrives on a tractor-trailer

so that Harry and the builders can build higher levels.

To make sure the scaffolding is safe the clamps are made tight.

Once the scaffolding is up, safety screens are fixed around the sides.

Accidents can happen... Harry and his friends must wear hard hats.

The roof beams are delivered by a special tractor-trailer...

...that lifts them up easily onto the scaffolding.

While each roof beam is held steady it is nailed into place.

Plywood strips are nailed to the beams and roofing felt laid over.

When it rains Harry and his friends have to stop work.

This is how tiles are laid:

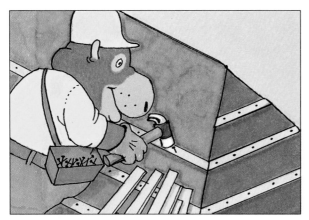

Strips are fixed on the roof felt.

Tiles are nailed so they overlap.

Ridge tiles cover the joints.

Gutters take away rain that
runs down the roof.

One roofer lays out
the tiles and another
nails them in place.

Now there is work for the carpenters
to do inside the house.

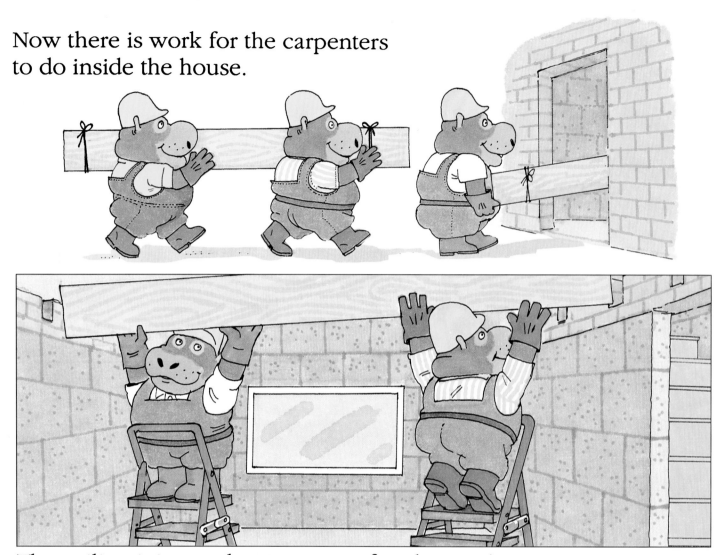

The ceiling joists and staircase are fixed into place.

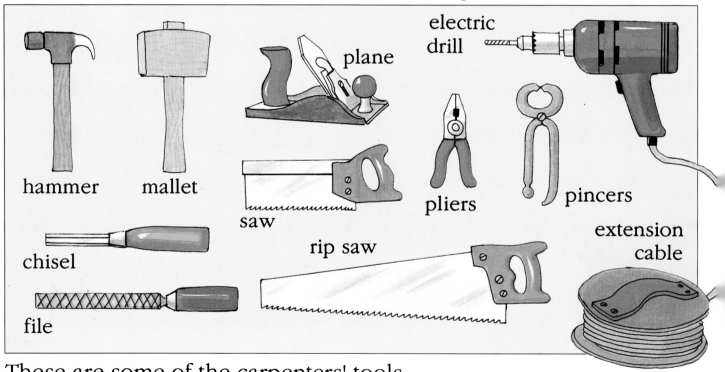

hammer   mallet   plane   electric drill

saw   pliers   pincers

chisel   rip saw   extension cable

file

These are some of the carpenters' tools.

Floorboards are fitted onto the joists, but not
before the electrician has put in the underfloor wiring.

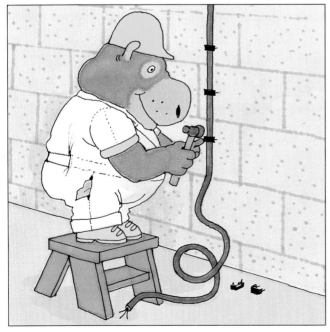

He fixes the electric wires to
the concrete block walls,

then screws plugs to the wires.
Later, he fits the lights.

The plumber has many jobs to do. Here are some of the things he will fix into place.

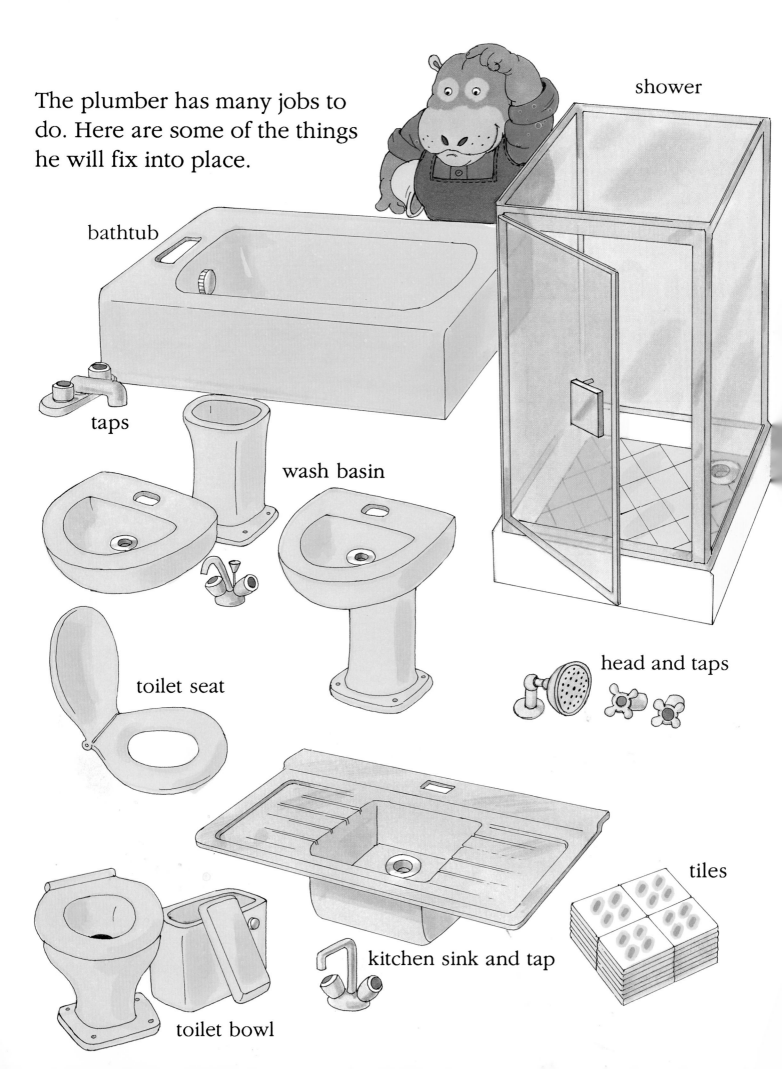

shower

bathtub

taps

wash basin

head and taps

toilet seat

toilet bowl

kitchen sink and tap

tiles

Metal pipes are measured, cut to size, and bent. These carry hot and cold water to the bathroom and the kitchen.

There is a lot of drilling

and fitting to do.

Taps are fitted, and the walls are tiled to protect them from splashes.

Pipes bring cold water to the kitchen and bathroom. The hot water tank heats it for warm baths and washing dishes.

These are the pipes that carry waste
water away from inside the house.

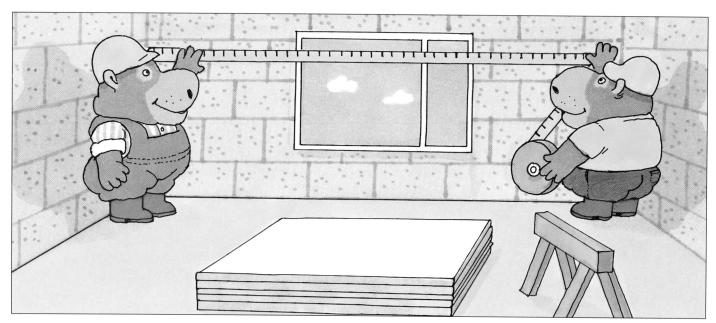

Now the house is nearly finished.
Sheetrock is measured and cut to
fit the cement block walls.
Holes are left for the
electrical fittings
to be finished off.

The sheetrock is fitted and nailed to the cement block walls.

The joints between the plaster board are covered over. The last plugs are then fitted.

Harry Hippo and his friends have finished the job. Now the house that Harry built can be sold.